MUSK OX BABIES
Of the Far North

Written by Helen von Ammon
Illustrations by Erin Mauterer

DOODLEBUG BOOKS • SAN FRANCISCO

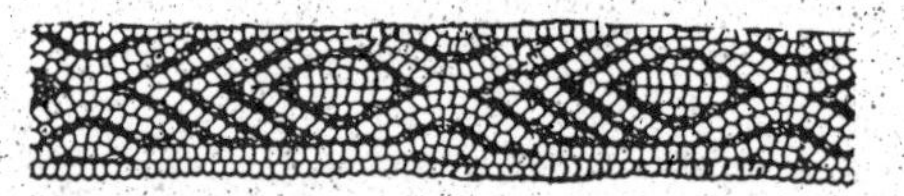

Doodlebug Books
48 San Antonio Place
San Francisco, CA 94133-4054 USA

Printed in the United States of America
Cover design by Erin Marie Mauterer
Book design by
Bluewater Advertising & Design
Ocean, New Jersey

10 9 8 7 6 5 4 3 2 1

Library of Congress Cataloging-in-Publication Data
von Ammon, Helen. Musk Ox Babies of the Far North/text by Helen von Ammon:
Illustrations by Erin M. Mauterer. 1st ed. p. cm.

ISBN 0-9647756-5-4

1. Musk Ox, Fiction (1. Animals—Fiction. 2. Alaska—Non-fiction):
2. Qiviut—Spinning & Knitting. I. Mauterer, Erin Marie, ill. II. Title.

CIP
96-096232

This book is printed on Recycled paper

INTRODUCTION

A spinning wheel turned fluffy white mounds of wool into yarn at a Florida county fair in the Fall of 1978. The spinner then knitted her yarn into beautiful sweaters. Intrigued by this tactile medium, I learned to spin not only wool but exotic fibers such as Mongolian baby camel down, cashmere, silk, angora, alpaca, llama and, most exciting of all, qiviut, one of the rarest fibers on earth.

Qiviut (kiv-ee-oot) is the soft underdown beneath ankle length brown/black guard hair on male and female musk oxen. Qiviut keeps musk oxen warm in the harsh Arctic climate of 50 degrees below zero Fahrenheit. Spinning and knitting this wondrous fiber of the Far North proved to me its superb qualities of lightweight warmth and natural, smoky-gray color. Almost overnight my life as a painter, exhibited in the United States and abroad, was eclipsed by exotic fibers and became my enduring passion. To learn more about qiviut and the mammals which produce it, I joined a team of volunteer workers at Large Animal Research Station in Fairbanks, Alaska where musk oxen, caribou and reindeer are studied. Fossils have proven the existence of musk oxen during the Pleistocene or Ice Age, some two million years ago. Musk oxen became extinct in Alaska in the 1800s and the worldwide population was believed to be about 5,000 animals. This near extinction signaled an urgency to preserve musk oxen habitats despite human encroachment, oil and mineral exploration. Through foresight, financial assistance, perseverance, dedication and physical effort the 34 musk ox calves which were transplanted from Greenland to Alaska in 1930 have ensured that this unique mammal will not again be endangered by man.

One of my assignments at Large Animal Research Station was minute-by-minute observation of several musk oxen in a harem. From a wooden observation tower ten feet off the ground, I observed with field glasses every movement of a bull, cows and their calves in a large pen below the tower. This computer-recorded data was later deciphered and studied by scientists. One cold September night from midnight to four a.m., temperature 36 degrees, I wrote:

NOTES FROM THE TOWER

"It is quiet and very dark except for a ribbon of pink fog which floats above distant Fairbanks. Observation flood lights reveal light, misty rain. All my musk oxen sleep. I ask myself, 'Do musk oxen dream?' As they sleep with legs extended, sometimes their four white furry ankles swim in the air. Are they nocturnally retracing the steps of their ancestors across the Bering Land Bridge - Siberia to Alaska? While he slumbers, the 800 pound bull shatters the silent night with a deep guttural, lion-like roar. He awakens, heaves himself up and looks around. Satisfied that all is well in his harem, he shifts his great mountain of fur back to the ground with ungainly grace and sleeps in earnest. Raindrops on the roof mingle with clicking sounds of caribou leg sinews. In a nearby pen, caribou pace pasture perimeters repeatedly in an endless migration. Their sleepy, restless babies grunt pig-like, 'Oink, oink, oink.' As if gentle music had been programmed, a Bach chorale plays softly on my small radio as sparrows chatter in green conifers and golden birch trees. Rex, a little calf, eats hungrily at the hay feeder, oblivious to the serenity and beauty of this hour. The world I came from seems remote, and I am deeply aware of being very happy."

A nightly yearning in Alaska was to see the aurora borealis for the first time. One frosty cold night during my watch in the observation tower, a bright moon dimmed the stars of the Big Dipper - I saw it! A greenish, pale veridian, eerie light arced East and West far into the sky. Bach's great organ toccata soared through my mind, appropriate for this glorious sight. The northern lights performed superbly different spectacles on several nights before my return to the "real" world in California.

Obsessed with musk oxen, I've returned again and again to the Large Animal Research Station, Fairbanks, and the Musk Ox Development Corporation's Musk Ox Farm in Palmer, Alaska. All MODC qiviut is machine spun into 100% qiviut yarn. Native Americans knit this yarn into lacy garments from patterns exclusive to each knitter's village and some are located in very remote Alaska. This Musk Ox Project has been in place for about thirty years with third and fourth generations of hand knitters. Knitters work from diagrams, and are paid by the stitch. Knitting is frequently the sole income for Eskimo families. These soft, beautiful scarves, tunics, hats and other warm garments are marketed from Anchorage by Oomingmak, one of the oldest Native cooperatives in the United States. While a volunteer at these two musk ox farms I've combed and sorted qiviut, collected urine for laboratory analysis, raked pens, picked lichen for winter musk ox treats, watched the wobbly first steps of newborns, cuddled and comforted sick calves and bottle fed them. Musk ox calves are endearingly shy and enchanting to watch as they play like puppies.

Except for the anthropomorphism, the facts herein are true based on my observations at the Musk Ox Farm in Palmer, Alaska and the Large Animal Research Station in Fairbanks, Alaska. I am grateful to the scientists, animal handlers and friends for sharing their experience and knowledge to my endless questions over the years.

Helen von Ammon
September 1996

NORTH POLE!
FAIRBANKS & PALMER
ALASKA
CANADA

CHAPTER 1

Snuggle into your very warmest clothes. Look at the map and find the North Pole, the top of the world. Brrrrr, this is the coldest place on earth. Icy winds blow hard and everywhere snow dazzles your eyes. Now look at the middle of the map and find Alaska. Alaska is such a big state it's called the "Great Land." Folks who live in the Great Land speak about far away places like New York, California and Texas, as the "Lower 48." Winters in Alaska are almost as cold as the North Pole so Spring and Summer are the best times to visit Unni and Chaun. Unni and Chaun are musk ox cows, born six years ago on an animal farm far north in Alaska.

CHAPTER 2

It was a warm, sunny May afternoon in Fairbanks, Alaska. Unni and Chaun munched their way slowly across the large pasture of green grass. They were good friends and shared the pasture with other cows awaiting the birth of their calves. Usually content to rest and thoughtfully ruminate (chew their cud, as cows do), today Unni and Chaun restlessly paced the fence perimeter. Each cow laid down, got up, only to do the same thing over and over again. Then Unni stopped pacing and spread her hind legs. Soon two tiny front hooves appeared from her furry behind, then a little wet nose, and soon a male calf plopped wetly onto the grass. At birth he was covered all over with brown fur and looked like a bear cub. So Unni named him Bear.

A couple of minutes later Chaun stood still, and with rear legs apart, her female calf was born. Chaun thought, "I've had a calf every Spring since I was four years old. I must name my new baby something easy to remember. 'Beth' sounds nice and is easy to say." And so she named her calf Beth.

Mama Unni and Mama Chaun licked their calves from nose to tiny tail, nuzzled the babies and encouraged them to stand. Although she wobbled about for a few minutes, little Beth hungrily sought and found her mother's udder of warm, rich milk.

Bear tried to stand but his newborn legs collapsed. Unni repeatedly nuzzled and licked him. Soon the earth stopped moving and when he shakily stood up, he was about as tall as the seat on a small tricycle. He was very hungry. All that flopping down and getting up on his new legs was confusing. Instinctively he knew lunch was here some place so he tried to squeeze between Unni's back legs to find her udder. But musk oxen's hind legs are knock-kneed. That means the knee bones turn in toward each other. So there wasn't room for Bear, small as he was, to go through the back door. Unni patiently, gently pushed him under her long skirt of fur and soon he got it right. He suckled long and greedily.

In the large maternity pasture with Unni, Bear, Chaun and Beth were five other cows who had not yet given birth to their calves. One cow said to the other cow nearby, "What do you suppose is going on over there with Unni and Chaun? I wonder if their babies have come. I'll stroll over and see." The curious cow looked down at the new babies. Bear, curled up like a big brown furry caterpillar, was taking a nap. The inquisitive cow said, "Unni's calf is hardly bigger than a soccer ball. I wonder if it will roll downhill?" With her large head, the cow roughly nudged Bear. Rudely awakened, Bear uncurled himself, stood up and said to the strange cow, "Why did you do that? I'm not a ball; I'm just a little calf." Unni rushed to him and with her long, upturned horns, she pushed away the jealous cow. "Bear, that cow is envious that you are the first calf to be born this Spring. She won't bother you again. Come and have some nice warm milk."

CHAPTER 3

Farm manager Bob talked to helpers Ray and Kathy as they approached the pasture where all calves would be born this year. "It's very important that we handle all newborn calves as little as possible. If one is ill and must receive a lot of treatment, the calf will keep a human scent and the mother will probably abandon her calf. Sometimes a cow who is a mother for the first time fails to take care of her baby. Then we must take the calf away from her. Whether rejected or abandoned the calf must be bottle fed musk ox milk or milk replacement." Kathy remembered last year, "We had to bottle raise Chinook. Newborn calves are covered with thick, dark brown fur which makes me want to cuddle them like a teddy bear but they are so very shy. Bottle feeding a little calf is such a wonderful, loving experience, but it takes a lot of time and work."

They entered the maternity pen to treat Bear and Beth.. Bob began talking to Unni in a calm, quiet voice. "Unni, do you remember last year right after your calf was born, we took him away from you for a couple of minutes. You were very upset when I picked him up and he struggled so hard I had to hold him tightly. But soon he was back at your side. Now, just like last year, it's very important that during the first two or three hours of Bear's life we take him away from you for just a couple of minutes. We want your calf to grow up healthy and strong. So we must swab his belly button with iodine, examine him quickly and see how much he weighs. I understand Unni, you are a good musk ox mother, and always are very protective of your calves."

Bob had been her friend and handler ever since Unni had been born on the farm six years ago. She trusted Bob and continued to listen. "You challenge everyone you believe may harm your baby, so Ray is carrying a big wooden board. He holds the board in front of you to protect me from your sharp horns when I pick up Bear." Unni had forgotten about last year's calf and just wanted these three humans out of her pasture. But Bob continued, "All newborn musk ox calves are frightened and wiggle wildly when someone picks them up. We handle them as little as possible."

Kathy placed the bathroom-type scale on the ground. Bob caught Bear and held him belly side up while Kathy gently rubbed the umbilical cord area (his belly button) with iodine to prevent infection. Bob held the furiously struggling calf in his arms and stepped on the scale. With patience and experience he examined Bear quickly. Setting the little calf back on the ground he smiled at the anxious mother, "There you are Unni, he's all yours. Just as I promised, it only took a couple of minutes." Bob weighed himself and announced to Kathy who recorded the information, "Bear weighs a healthy 24 pounds." They used the same procedure for Beth who weighed 20 pounds. Ray put away his wooden shield, glad that no one had been injured. The threesome left the pasture and all would watch for the birth of the next calf. Then they would return to repeat the procedure for each new baby.

This was Bear's first contact with humans and he was completely confused to be among all the curious cows who had gathered around Unni. He asked himself, "Which of these cows is Mama Unni? They're all covered with shiny fur which almost touches the ground. All of them have long horns which turn up at the ends." He trotted over to Chaun who was nearest him. Chaun knew immediately that Bear was not her calf. She wasn't very polite when she pushed him away with her head. Unni was still upset at all the commotion but she quickly found her wandering calf. Gently she sniffed him to make sure it was Bear, then nuzzled her baby. Bear felt much better after a snack of Unni's milk.

Musk ox mothers are very tolerant of their offspring and allow the calves to play their favorite little tricks. Beth laughed at Bear. He looked so funny when he stood close to Unni and sucked the upturned tip of one of her beautiful horns.

When Chaun rested, Beth liked to climb atop her mother's neck. Then she slid down the furry slope. When Chaun was tired of the game, she arose to nibble fresh green grass and Beth trotted along close to her. Chaun told her, "For about a month after birth, healthy musk ox calves gain about one pound a day. Soon you will be too big to play this baby game."

CHAPTER 4

Winters in musk ox land are almost as cold as the North Pole. Bob mentioned to Kathy, "The weather is unpredictable here in Alaska and sometimes Spring comes in March or as late as June. Don't put away your parka and rubber boots just yet. Last May we had snow storms every day for a week. The sun came out at last and melted the snow into a muddy, gooey mess." Kathy was enthusiastic anyway, "I'm ready for Spring and warm sunshine all day and almost all night. The cherry trees will be so happy to welcome the sun and snowy petals will blossom overnight. Gentle winds will blow pale pink petals everywhere. Before the drifting petals hide in the pasture grass, the calves will comically try to catch them."

Beth commented to Bear, "Have you noticed that our mothers have begun to look different?" Bear looked at Unni and Chaun, "They do look funny. Their fur is almost falling off in great big chunks. Look at my fur, is mine loose like that?" The two calves examined each other's thick and soft, dark brown coat. Beth reasoned, "No fur is falling off. We must be too young to have that much fur. Look, a piece of Mama Chaun's fur about as big as my hoof just blew off and landed over there. I'm curious, let's go look. It's greyish brown, soooo soft and light. I wonder who named us 'musk' oxen; that sounds like a bad smell. This fur has a faint, almost sweet smell." Later Beth would learn the fur was called "qiviut" and in a couple of months Beth and Bear also would grow short coats of qiviut.

They watched a slight breeze lift up the small, light piece of downy fur as if it were a feather. The qiviut danced with the wind and turned somersaults up and down. The calves watched it drift silently over the fence. Bear remembered, "That must be the same kind of fur that tickles my nose when I drink Mama Unni's milk. That reminds me - I'm hungry."

CHAPTER 5

Bob and Kathy came into the cows' pasture and Bob spoke to Unni and Chaun about plans for the day. "Good morning, ladies. Now that your calves have been born we can comb off all that qiviut which kept you warm during this past winter." Bob pronounced the strange word *kiv-ee-oot*. Bear wondered, "What does qiviut mean?" As if he had heard Bear's question, Bob said "Qiviut is an Eskimo word which means underdown or underwool."

He continued, "Last winter was especially cold - sometimes the temperature was 50 degrees below zero. It's Spring now so you won't need your underdown any more this year. You will grow another winter coat when it gets cold. Last year each of you gave us five and a half pounds of qiviut. Since our past winter was very cold, maybe this year when we comb you from head to your tiny tail we will get even more qiviut. Do you know that your fur is very valuable and that it's one of the most rare fibers on earth? Spinners buy your qiviut from our farm. They spin it into yarn and then knit or weave the yarn into lightweight, warm clothing. The money they pay us for qiviut buys your favorite treat of grain, and pays our expenses of taking such good care of you."

Bob, Kathy and Ray worked together to bring the animals into the big red barn. Kathy said, "The animals aren't too happy about coming from the fresh air of their pasture into the confinement of the barn. But they are used to it because we bring them in often for Dr. Black's tests, examinations and to be weighed. They come willingly, but without enthusiasm. And they expect grain treats for their cooperation." Kathy walked up to Unni and said, "You know grain is irresistible to all you musk oxen, just as chocolate is to me." Tantalizingly she rattled the can of tempting grain. Kathy walked backwards leading Unni who greedily guzzled the grain. Bear trotted along close to Mama Unni. Before entering the barn, Unni walked through a narrow chute and stepped on a floor scale. Outside the chute Ray recorded her weight at 425 pounds.

Unni continued the short distance into the barn and entered the narrow metal stanchion to be combed, as she had done every Spring. Unni said to herself, "The handlers know I can make a terrible fuss if I want to while I'm being held in this stanchion even though it doesn't hurt me. It holds my body still so they can comb off my qiviut but I can still move my head. If they keep the grain bucket filled outside the stanchion where I can reach it, I'll behave nicely. This new volunteer, Ellen, said she will comb the qiviut off my face. I hate for people to touch my muzzle." Ellen, eager to save all available qiviut, placed her comb on Unni's forehead. Unni was annoyed. She swung her great head upward and abruptly dumped Ellen on the cold cement floor. As Unni munched grain her attitude improved and the combers quickly harvested her qiviut, but took none between her horns.

Mary, who often helped on the farm after school, and Ellen combed Unni's left side and Ray combed her right side. They used wide-toothed combs of plastic or metal, like large dog grooming combs. Musk oxen seem calmer when their handlers speak gently to them. So Mary talked to Unni while they combed. "Did you know that there is a Musk Ox Farm in Palmer, Alaska? They have more musk oxen than we have here in Fairbanks. All their qiviut is used by Native Americans, sometimes we call them Eskimos. These women earn money for their families by hand knitting beautiful lacy scarves, warm baby hats and lots of other garments. The designs are all different because they use patterns from their native villages. The Eskimo women teach their daughters to knit traditional patterns, and the daughters teach their daughters. All those musk oxen must be very proud that they can help these Eskimo families."

The three combers worked swiftly and soon they had great sheets of Unni's qiviut piled into two big plastic bags. Mary weighed and wrote down six pounds of qiviut Unni had provided. Ray opened the heavy stanchion gate with a loud **CLANG!** and Unni rushed through the open barn door into brilliant sunshine.

Led into the barn following the refilled grain can, Chaun was weighed, and willingly entered the stantion to be combed. Chaun behaved like a lady. . . as long as the big, black plastic bucket was filled with grain. When the bucket was empty, irritably she tossed the empty bucket across the room with her great horns to demand "More grain!" As soon as Chaun's muzzle was deep in the refilled grain bucket, the combers quickly relieved her of two huge bags of qiviut. Ray flung open the barn door, clanged open the stanchion, and Chaun dashed outside.

Both cows were happy to be out of the barn and felt frisky without the six pounds of qiviut each had provided. Unni commented to Chaun, "It seemed a long time that I was in the barn. I'll be so glad to see Bear and I know he will be hungry." Chaun was worried, "But neither of our calves is outside waiting for us. *Where are our babies?!*"

CHAPTER 6

While Unni and Chaun were being combed, Kathy had led Bear and Beth into another part of the barn. They entered a small, white wooden stall with walls as high as Kathy's shoulders. The shy calves backed away from her until their rumps were pressed hard against the wall of the stall. Bear tried to act bravely but he was so frightened he couldn't close his eyes, and his legs wobbled. Beth was terrified and hid her muzzle in Bear's rump fur. Kathy sat with the calves on the clean cement floor of the stall and talked soothingly to them. "Don't be afraid. As soon as you 'go' I'll catch the urine in these two little plastic bottles. Then Bob will come with a syringe. A syringe is a narrow plastic tube which measures a small amount of liquid. Bob will use the syringe to take a small blood sample from both of you. I promise it's not going to hurt; you won't even feel it. Our laboratory will analyze the urine and blood and tell us whether you are as healthy as we think you are. You want to grow big and handsome like your mother and father, don't you?"

Unni and Chaun waited impatiently outside the barn for their calves who were still in the barn. Separated from their babies, the disappointed cows repeatedly roared and sounded like lions in a zoo. Up and down, back and forth they paced the length of the pasture. Their ferocious roaring could be heard all over the farm. Their mothers'

anxious calls frightened the little calves even more. They feared something terrible was happening outside. Bear was so nervous he forgot how hungry he was. In a tree just outside the barn, a quarrelsome gray squirrel ran up and down, round and round his tree. Greatly disturbed and anxious, he flicked and twitched his long fluffy tail. He was so angry his teeth chattered constantly. This tree was the squirrel's home and all the roaring and commotion nearby made him very upset. He screeched as loud as he could at the roaring cows, "I'm just a small squirrel but I have rights too, y'know. How can anybody sleep around here? Stop making all that noise!"

The cows ignored his bad-tempered tantrum and roared even louder. Wildly they ran up and down the pasture, fearful that their babies were being harmed. Still in the barn, the calves could hold out no longer; they had to 'go.' Kathy filled their urine specimen bottles and left the stall. Beth whispered to Bear, "She was so nice, I even let her stroke my fur and pet me. I wish she had stayed and talked to us." The stall door opened and Bob towered over the little calves. Beth's voice quavered in a whisper, "Here's Bob with his instruments of torture. I know it's going to hurt." Bear was too scared to cry *baaa*. And there was nowhere to run and hide. He couldn't look at Bob and the awful syringe. Bob hadn't yet touched him, but Bear already knew it hurt.

Carefully, quickly Bob inserted the syringe needle under Beth's soft, brown fur. Before she knew it, the syringe was half full and Bob said, "Thank you, Beth, you're all done." He did the same to Bear and left the stall. Now that the ordeal was over Bear laughed and bragged, "That wasn't bad at all. Did you notice how brave I was?"

Suddenly the stall door was opened wide. Bear and Beth raced outside to their mothers in the warm, sunlit pasture. Relieved to be reunited with their babies, Unni and Chaun immediately stopped their anxious roaring to sniff and nuzzle their calves. The cows hurried away from the big red barn as Bear and Beth happily trotted along.

CHAPTER 7

Calves are especially full of energy in the late afternoon and play like large frisky puppies. Beth was Bear's favorite playmate. She was taking a nap so Bear tickled her muzzle with his nose. Her big brown eyes looked at him drowsily, "I'll play later, Bear, I'm just too comfortable and warm snuggled up to Mama Chaun." Bear bounded off independently muttering, "Phooey! If no one wants to play I can amuse myself." He had watched male musk oxen butt heads in a far pasture and now he tried to copy their behavior. He butted a post, backed off, nibbled grass, then butted the post again. Beth sometimes let Bear butt heads with her. She knew he wasn't trying to hurt her; he was practicing to be a grown-up, big bull some day.

Bear wandered across the pasture and came upon two calves. "Why are you two calves digging near the fence?" Bear asked. The calves were too busy to answer so Bear decided to investigate. He joined the excavation team and all three calves vigorously dug and dug with their tiny hooves. Soon there was a hole in the ground big enough for a baby musk ox to slither under the fence.

Bear still didn't know why they were digging and it bored him anyway. "Whew!" he gasped. "This is exhausting work!" The calves agreed. And all three of them collapsed in a single jumble of slumbering dark brown fur and twelve furry white legs.

Later that afternoon, after a nap, Bear was ready to play again. "Come on, Beth, I'll race you around the pasture." He especially liked to play this game with Beth because he almost always won. After declaring himself the winner, he ran to the top of a small hill and dared Beth, "I'll bet you can't push me off this hill." Beth thought, "This is such a silly game, Bear just wants to show me how strong he is." Anyway, she humored him and declared loudly, "Bear, King of the Mountain."

CHAPTER 8

Bear had watched cows scratch their rumps on the metal water trough. Although he didn't understand why they did it, he copied their behavior and rubbed his little behind on the trough. Many times Beth watched Mama Chaun at the water trough. Her shiny, dark brown guard hair remained although Chaun had been combed of her qiviut underdown. The long guard hair almost touched the ground and was hot and itchy so she scratched her rump on the metal water trough. Then she put her white, furry front hoof in the cool water and sighed, "My, that feels good."

Chaun dipped her muzzle in the water and drank slowly. As she raised her head, streams of water dripped from her furry face. Beth hadn't tried to drink because the trough was too high for small calves to reach the water. One day Beth said to herself, "There's a low platform beside the trough. It's just high enough for little calves to get their muzzles into the water without falling into the trough. I'm going to climb up there and drink just like Mama. It must be good because she does this a lot." Beth dipped her mouth in the water and waited for it to taste good. It didn't taste like anything at all. "I don't understand why Mama likes this stuff. It's just BLAH. Mama's milk is much better." Beth continued to visit the water trough with Mama Chaun and drank a little water. She soon learned, "Water is pretty good, especially when Mama won't hold still when I want to nurse."

Kathy welcomed Chuck, a new volunteer. "Volunteers are very important on musk ox farms. We greatly appreciate your energy, enthusiasm and willingness to help where we need you. Sometimes comical situations occur." Kathy laughed as she recalled one incident. "All musk oxen love lichen as much as humans enjoy ice cream, and volunteers are happy to pick it for them on nearby hills. I took a group of volunteers to a hillside which is thickly covered with greyish-green lichen. One energetic lady enthusiastically stuffed her burlap sack full to the top with moist lichen. She tried to lift the heavy bag onto her shoulder but its weight pulled her over backwards. Flat on her back she giggled and squealed, arms and legs waving around wildly like a turtle on its back. The lichen-covered hill was so soft and damp she couldn't get up. We all had a good laugh then pulled her to her feet."

Chuck was tall, muscular, very confident of his ability to work with horses. Musk oxen were a new experience for him and casually he entered the cows' pasture. He watched Chaun slowly approach the water trough. Kathy was in the pasture filling the hay feeder. Chuck commented to her, "Musk oxen walk in such a deliberate, slow, plodding way. They must be very clumsy animals." Kathy said nothing but smiled at his inaccurate observation. On this hot July day Chuck would learn something surprising about musk oxen.

Chaun was wary of newcomers to her pasture. "I heard Chuck's silly remark that musk oxen are clumsy. I'll just check him out." As Chuck faced her, the 425 pound cow suddenly charged toward him with the speed of a locomotive. Head lowered, upturned horns extended, menacingly her eyes were fixed on her target only yards away.

Chuck was horrified with fright at the sudden change in the "clumsy" musk ox. Powerless to move from her path, he froze. One inch from Chuck's big brass belt buckle, Chaun suddenly stopped in front of her target. Unwaveringly, she stared at him for a moment to enjoy the effect of her charge. Then she turned and plodded slowly, deliberately away from her frightened foe. But Chaun hadn't finished Chuck's lesson on respect for musk oxen. After he had recovered from his heart-stopping experience, Chuck filled the big water trough. He held the long, green water hose over the metal trough and allowed it to overflow so that the animals would have cool, clean water. Intent on his job, he faced the trough, his back to the cows in the pasture. Chaun, in her plodding way, walked toward the water trough as Beth followed. Chaun still resented Chuck's untrue remark about her species. She whispered to Beth, "Remember how Chuck said we are clumsy? He's going to regret saying that." Slowly, without a sound, Chaun walked up close to Chuck's backside. The gushing water made lots of noise so he didn't hear her approach. Chaun lowered her immense head. With a swift, forceful upward movement, she butted Chuck squarely on the behind. Cowboy hat, boots and all, forcefully she pushed him head first into the water trough with a drenching S P L A S H ! Beth jumped up and down with laughter. Chaun chuckled mischievously, "I enjoyed that!"

CHAPTER 9

Musk oxen don't have a lot to do in their pastures except gossip, eat grass, rest and ruminate contentedly. Rumen is fodder eaten earlier, then later brought up to chew at leisure from the first of their four stomachs. So musk oxen have plenty of time to devise their own amusements and have developed a unique sense of humor. Chaun had been bored while she waited eight months for Beth to be born. She had quickly gobbled up her treat of grain. Now she stared at the big, empty grain bucket. It was about two feet across, of soft, black plastic. She commented to Unni, who was also bored, "I have a knack for using my horns. Watch this." She speared her left horn into the bucket, lifted it high above her head and twirled it in the air, faster and faster. Then she flung it to the fence five yards away. Repeatedly Chaun twirled and tossed the bucket which by now was quite beaten up. Unni complemented her, "That was wonderful. I have a trick I sometimes do on cold mornings. Watch." Unni ran swiftly around the fence perimeter. Suddenly she jumped up, all four legs and 425 pounds were off the ground. She turned mid-air in the opposite direction and made a safe landing. "A perfect ballet jump called a tour j'tet," Unni boasted proudly. Then, with her head held high, she walked back to Chaun with stately grace.

Musk oxen play unusual ball games. Bear butts a soccer ball with his head, then chases it. The other calves get the idea and join in. A friend gave Bob a huge beach ball of red, blue, yellow and green. Bob wondered, "These male musk oxen have never seen a big round, brightly colored ball. I'll toss it into the pasture and watch their reactions. Here goes." He pitched the ball into the large pasture where eight bulls were grazing.

The biggest bull wondered, "What is this unusual new object in our pen? Since I'm the strongest bull here, I'll touch the thing lightly with one of my big horns." The ball rolled swiftly downhill and gathered speed. The colors whirled and blended which made it look even more strange. "This odd thing didn't injure Dominant Bull," said another bull, "I'll push it from the opposite side."

Soon all eight bulls gathered around, fascinated with this new toy. Bob laughed, "I'll throw the ball again far into their pasture and watch." Snorting with excitement, these 700 to 800 pound males, their long, hairy skirts flying, wildly chased the colorful ball. As long as Bob threw it they dashed crazily after the ball. At last Bob reluctantly stopped the game. "I can't play with you guys all day; I've got chores to do. One last toss and you're on your own." He threw the ball far into the pasture. It took only a few seconds for the big bulls to learn they could push the ball uphill with their huge heads and comically, wildly chase it as it rolled downhill.

CHAPTER 10

Bear was curious about everything. Sometimes it got him in trouble. "Beth, this green gate is huge and heavy; what do you suppose is on the other side of it?" "I know what you're thinking, Bear. You're so small you can probably squirm under the gate. But forget it! If our nice caretakers had wanted us to be on the other side they would have opened the gate for us." Having firmly stated her advice to Bear, Beth walked primly to a spot of soft, fresh grass, tucked her legs beneath her and watched Bear get himself into trouble.

Sensible advice always challenged Bear. He couldn't resist the temptation to explore. Peevishly he muttered, "I hope Bob isn't around. Sometimes he yells at me for the silliest things. Like the time we three calves dug a big hole under the pasture fence. We could have escaped easily, but we didn't. So what's the big deal! I wasn't even the one who started digging, but I got the blame anyway. He made such a fuss, right in front of the other calves. It was so embarrassing. When he goes on like that I have to look up at him innocently, as if I'm begging to be cuddled. Then he calms down." With a sly grin, Bear looked right and left—Bob was nowhere in sight. With a delighted, "Good!" Bear proceeded with his plan to explore the other side of the big green fence.

Bear flattened himself on his belly; his four little legs wiggled, squiggled and struggled. Slowly he inched his body under the gate—success!. Delighted with his prank, he laughed, "I did it! Come on, Beth, it's easy." "No," she said, "this time I'm not going to play your dumb game. You'll be in big trouble if Bob catches you." Bear happily pranced round and around, ran up and down outside the big gate. Very pleased with himself, he boasted, "What a clever calf I am." After a while he stopped his silly antics and said, "Daring adventures always make me hungry. Let's go get breakfast." Suddenly he realized that breakfast was inside the gate and he was *outside*.
"No problem," he bragged, "I'll just squeeze myself back under the gate." He tried to make himself small. He struggled, squirmed and squiggled, pushed unsuccessfully with his front legs, then turned around and tried to push his rear end under the gate. Still no luck. He muttered, "I couldn't have gotten bigger in such a short time." But he just couldn't make himself small enough. Beth watched his struggles and smirked, "You should have taken my advice. Just wait 'til Bob catches you." Bear could see Mama Unni quietly munching grass in the far pasture. Then, folding her legs beneath her, she rested and dozed off. Bear whined, "How could my mother forget about me - especially when I'm so hungry!" Beth was no comfort, "See, I told you so. Now you're in trouble. What are you going to do? I can't help you, and Bob may come along any minute."

By this time Bear was very upset. He cried, "Baaa, baaaa." Not a cow or calf in the pasture even looked up. Louder he cried, "Baaa, baaa, **BAAA!** Unni heard her calf's cries and anxiously looked around for him. She was desperate to find her baby and asked Chaun whether she had seen him. Chaun was sympathetic, "I don't see him anywhere. But it sounds as if he is over there near the big gate." Unni walked toward his bleating which became louder and louder. Horrified, she found him *outside* the gate.

There was nothing she could do to get him back where he belonged. In her anxiety, she poked her long horns through the wide bars of the gate. That was as close as she could get to Bear.

Mary was raking a nearby pasture and heard the pitiful baaas of a young calf. Immediately she dropped her rake and rushed to see what had happened. She understood the dilemma at once but there was still another problem. Unni stood protectively beside Bear, separated from him by the gate. Mary spoke quietly, "Unni, try to understand, I didn't do this to Bear, it was his curiosity. But I'll try to get him back to you. If you could just put your horns away it would be easier for me." Mary looked around for help but no one was within shouting distance. Although she could use Bob's help, she hoped he would not come along just now. She knew he would scold Bear for his newest prank.

Unni's menacing horns poked between the bars of the gate. Mary strained her head as far back from the sharp horns as possible. Bear stopped his baas and thought, "I don't like to have humans pick me up. But I'm in trouble and maybe she can help. Besides, I'm very hungry. I will resist her efforts to pick me up and I'll struggle just enough that she will understand I'm not a calf to be cuddled under normal circumstances." Unni and Bear were very upset so Mary kept talking to them soothingly. Finally she said, "I gotcha, Bear, but if you keep struggling like a big furry worm, I may drop you. I'm just folding your little legs under you. Now I'm pushing you under the gate as hard as I can. **Ooooph!** Therrrrre you go, Bear. You're back in the pasture where you belong. Try not to get into any more trouble at least for today. I've had enough excitement for a while."

With great relief, Mama Unni sniffed and licked her calf as they trotted far away from the gate. Mary smiled at their retreating furry behinds. "I'm happy I could help. Bear is such a cute and clever calf it's impossible to be mad at him."

CHAPTER 11

Shimmering green leaves of birch trees shade the far pasture where Beth and Chaun often rest with other cows and calves. Beth thought, "It's so cool and hilly here. It's the prettiest place I've ever seen. Mama Chaun has never taken me beyond this spot. On such a warm afternoon all my animal friends are sleeping. I'll just see what is farther back among the trees."

Alone for the first time in her young life, Beth ran up and down the small hills. It wasn't really such a large area but she sniffed every new smell and explored each grassy hill. Soon she was tired and tucked her furry little white legs beneath her body. Quickly she fell sound asleep and dreamed of Bear and their favorite games.

Later in the afternoon, high in the trees the joyful gossiping of many twittering sparrows awakened her. She stood up sleepily and looked around. "Where am I? I can't remember which way I came. Mama Chaun is nowhere around, and neither is Bear. I'm LOST! How could I have wandered so far without Mama. Bear would do something like this but I never do such dumb things."

A troubled calf's solution to any problem is to cry, "Baa, baaa, baaaa." But Beth didn't want to be a crybaby so timidly she tried just one "Baaa." Then louder, "BAAAA." No results. So as loud as she could she cried **"BAAAAA."**

Beyond a small hill Bear heard her baaaas and ran to her. "Beth," he said sternly, "Do be quiet! You sound like a lost goat. You'll awaken everyone." She ignored his unsympathetic comments and continued, "Baa, BAA, **BAAA.**" Bear didn't see any problem so he went back behind a small hill and resumed nibbling grass. Beth's cries awakened Chaun. In her dreams she had feasted endlessly on treats of fresh willow branches and grain. Groggily she walked over the hills toward the louder and more pitiful baaas. Cold, miserable and hungry, Beth thought, "Here comes some one. I'll cry louder. Baa, BAAA, BAAAA! Surely Mama Chaun will find me. It seems like I've been here forever."

Chaun walked through the dappled sunlight toward the increasingly frantic cries and found Beth lonely and frightened. She sniffed and calmed her baby by stroking Beth's small, quivering body with strokes of her pink tongue. Beth gratefully pressed her muzzle into Mama Chaun's long, thick fur coat. Happy to be together again, they joined musk ox cows and calves napping in the afternoon shade. Beth decided, "That's enough exploring. It's too scary. Besides, it makes me hungry."

CHAPTER 12

A big bus, yellow as a sunflower, rumbled noisily up the road one clear September afternoon. It stopped near a pasture of several cows and their calves. About thirty very energetic children exploded from the bus. They laughed, talked and yelled to each other despite the teachers' pleas, "Children, please, remember what we told you. You must be quiet or you will frighten the musk oxen we've come to see and learn about." The children, excited to be out of the classroom and on a field trip, remained noisy and ran toward the fence which separates visitors from the musk ox pasture. Immediately Unni and Chaun and the four other cows urgently called their calves. "Quickly, get in the center of our circle. All this noise means there is danger." The cows faced the boisterous crowd, their long, ivory-colored horns faced outward, ready to attack any enemy who approached them or their calves. The confused calves in the middle of the encircled cows wondered, "What is happening?" One calf was so confused he faced inside the circle with his rump exposed to the danger.

Bob began to speak and at last the children quieted down. He answered their questions. "These domesticated musk oxen are behaving as their ancestors have done for thousands of years. In the wild, bulls, cows and calves are grouped together in herds.

When they sense danger the bulls form the outside of a defensive circle, with cows and calves inside the ring. Musk oxen can usually fight off attacks from wolves, grizzly bears and polar bears by using their large, sharp, upturned horns. Unfortunately, this defense is not effective against guns." Bob led the children to another area and the frightened musk oxen disbanded their defense formation and resumed their quiet, gentle lives.

Chinook, a yearling (one year old calf) continued to graze near the fence and didn't join the cows and calves now resting after their frightening experience. Bob explained to the children, "Chinook's mom was new at motherhood and seemed to have no interest in feeding and caring for her baby. So Chinook was taken from her. Musk ox calves are normally extremely shy and fearful of people, but Chinook was bottle raised and received so much attention and love from his handlers that he became bold and fearless of people. As you see, relentlessly Chinook begs visitors for freshly cut willow branches." The children were delighted to poke branches to him through the fence. Chinook ate greedily until the children returned reluctantly to their bus. The bus rumbled off and from the back window one small boy waved good-bye all the way down the road.

CHAPTER 13

The long, green grass in the gently sloping far pasture had turned greenish-gold. It was time to make hay which musk oxen would eat through the winter when snow covered the land. Early one Autumn morning, Lanny came to the Research Station with three horses which would pull the haying machines. Beautiful, chocolate colored Belgians named Jack, Jill and Sally, the horses had long manes and tails like pale golden silk and their feet were big and furry. They were huge, much taller than Lanny and almost twice as big as musk ox cows which they now saw for the first time.

The musk oxen were, in city terms, a couple of blocks away from the horses. They grazed quietly in a large pasture surrounded by strong fences. Still, the horses were frightened by these unusual creatures of blockish shape, ankle length dark fur and long, upturned horns. The horses reared up, snorted and whinnied, and tried to get away from Lanny. He had a difficult time controlling them in their harnesses. At last Jack and Jill were calm, but Sally was still nervous. Excitedly she pulled away instead of forward each time a musk ox turned its massive head and ominous horns in her direction. Lanny's voice rang out urgently persuading and encouraging his team, "Step up, Sally; come around, Sally; good boy Jack." At last the grass was cut. Later the horses pulled a bright orange-colored machine. Noisily it picked up and digested the cut grass, then out it plopped it as hay, neatly tied in oblong bales with strong, thick cords.

Huge horses, noisy machines, and Lanny's loud commands, all were ignored by the musk oxen. Throughout the commotion they remained dignified and calm. Contemplatively they ruminated as if big, beautiful horses visited the farm every day.

CHAPTER 14

Bob and Kathy were discussing animal behavior on a late August morning before beginning their daily farm chores. Suddenly there was a very loud sound nearby, like great boulders clashing. It could be heard a mile away. They rushed to the far pasture which contained four large bulls. Cautiously, outside the fence, they watched two bulls violently butting heads. On impact, the mighty clash of their great stone-like head bosses was powerful and frightening. Bob remarked quietly, "Although male and female musk oxen have horns, bulls have a thick, stone-like horn formation atop the brain area called a 'boss.' This protects them somewhat from furious butting battles between males."

He continued, "During most of the year bulls ignore females and take no part in raising their calves. This time of year is the beginning of rut, the mating season, when male musk oxen become very interested in female musk oxen and challenge other bulls for territory and cows. Today we will set up the first harem of five cows and one bull. A cow is quite easy to coax into a pasture new to her. A container of grain is extended to the cow as the handler walks backwards down the level path to the cow's new location. A musk ox will follow a handler anywhere with its muzzle in a bucket of grain. After a day or two when the cows are accustomed to their new temporary location, we will bring in one bull."

Kathy commented, "During most of the year, bulls are usually big, powerful and stoic. They just want to graze, rest, enjoy life and the change of seasons. Rut certainly changes their dispositions and the bulls become disagreeable and really nasty. A bull guards his harem so jealously it is dangerous to be nearby. Last year I walked past Big Maak's harem which is surrounded by a heavy wooden fence. I certainly hadn't intended to make eye contact with him. But suddenly, through an open space in the fence, he and I were looking eye to eye. He thought I was challenging him and was he furious! Imagine me, Kathy, at 110 pounds, challenging an 800 pound bull! Before I could turn around and run, he violently charged the inside of the heavy wooden fence right where I stood. I thought for sure he would break through. My heart was stomping in my chest; I couldn't get away from there fast enough."

Bob decided which cows were to be in the first harem. "Unni and Chaun are such good friends we'll put them in first. Although they were weaned at three months of age, the calves will stay with their mothers in the harem.. Bear and Beth now eat grown up musk ox food. It contains all kinds of good things such as barley, corn, dried beet pulp, salt, molasses, vitamins and minerals, and now they are big enough to eat from the hay feeder. We will add three more cows after I carefully check their health and heredity records."

Bob also had a plan to get the bull into the harem without trouble. "Each pasture gate is locked along the path to the first harem. Even huge male musk oxen are curious about things unusual to them. The bull will soon learn that his gate has been left open. By himself the bull will wander up the path to his new harem of cows. Another keeper will open the harem gate and lock it quickly after he is inside." All went as Bob had carefully planned. Beth and Bear, now four months old, began a new experience.

CHAPTER 15

Horton, the bull chosen for the first harem, strolled into the pasture where five cows were quietly grazing and talking among themselves. Chaun mentioned to Beth, "Horton isn't as bad tempered as Big Maak but he isn't exactly sweet either. Look, he's already approaching Unni." Beth was about to take a nap but decided, "This is so exciting; I'll nap later. I've never seen a male musk ox except far off in the bull pasture. I wonder what will happen?" Later she and Bear would talk about everything.

Horton sniffed Unni's rump to learn whether she was in estrus. Estrus means that her body was ready to receive Horton's seed for making a new baby musk ox. Unni quickly walked away from Horton. Horton said to himself, "Unni can see I'm a huge, handsome musk ox with magnificent horns and a great horn boss. I won't take her rejection personally. She just isn't ready. I'll come back later." Then Horton grumbled, "Bear, that little calf of hers, is such a nuisance! He is so curious he watches everything and he's always in the way. Now he calmly nibbles at my hay feeder. I'll just show him who's boss." Bear munched hungrily and ignored the big bull. Horton walked over to him and with his great head, roughly pushed Bear away from his hay snack. Bear, surprised at such nasty behavior, thought, "I wonder what that was all about." Puzzled but unhurt later he returned to eat hay.

Horton went to Chaun, sniffed. Beth had never seen her mother with a male musk ox. She was frightened and thought, "Horton is so much bigger, taller than Mama Chaun and weighs about 800 pounds, almost twice as much as Mama. I hope he won't hurt us." Chaun didn't run from Horton but stood very still. In male musk ox language, this told him she was in estrus and he could proceed. Beth thought it best to watch from a safe distance so she quickly scampered away from her mother. In fearful silence she said, "Please, Mr. Horton, don't hurt Mama Chaun."

Immediately Horton raised himself on his back hooves to his great, majestic height. He was very close to Chaun's rump and placed his front hooves on her back. With quick forward motions, Horton planted his seed, called sperm, inside Chaun's body which was ready to receive and nourish it. Despite Horton's great body weight on her back, Chaun was not injured as the mating had taken no more than 20 seconds. She allowed Horton to repeat his mating motions several more times within five or ten minutes. During the rut when her body was in estrus, Unni and Horton also mated. Even though both male and female bodies were covered with thick, long guard hair the matings were successful. Horton's seed inside Chaun and Unni grew bigger and bigger until the following Spring. Then in April they became Mama Chaun and Mama Unni to wet and furry, healthy baby musk oxen.

By the time the new babies were born to Unni and Chaun, Beth and Bear were yearlings. In two or three more years Beth and Bear will mate and produce babies as musk oxen have done for thousands of years. Throughout their expected life span of about 18 years, Beth, Bear and their calves will receive devoted care on the musk ox farm. And all their babies will be endearingly shy and enchantingly beautiful.

THE GENTLE ART OF HELEN VON AMMON

Helen von Ammon's career with the Central Intelligence Agency posted her to Asia, Europe and the Middle East. Her lifelong passion for painting reflects this extensive travel. Some 16 years ago, Helen discovered the world of fiber and her handspun, handknit garments continue to be influenced by travel. She still "paints" with a palette of exotic fibers - silk, cashmere, angora, alpaca and most rare of all, qiviut. Qiviut (*kiv-ee-oot*) is the underdown which warms musk oxen during harsh Arctic winters. In the Spring, musk oxen shed their renewable qiviut and Helen goes to Alaska to comb this wondrous fiber, which she purchases in large quantities. She returns to her studios to translate this rare, lightweight fiber into unique, one-of-a-kind garments.

Helen von Ammon teaches creative design, spinning and knitting from Arizona to Australia, and is the author of *How To Spin A Rabbit*. She shares her San Francisco home with three charming English Angora rabbits who are happy to contribute their soft fur for Helen's cozy handknits.

ERIN MAUTERER has illustrated several children's books including *How To Spin A Rabbit* (Doodlebug Books). She lives in Ocean, New Jersey with her husband and two daughters.